EXPRESS NEWSPAPERS plc, Ludgate House,
245 Blackfriars Road,
London SE1 9UX.

Produced by Brainwaves Limited
5 Highwood Ridge, Hatch Warren, Basingstoke,
Hampshire RG22 4UU.

ISBN 0–85079–250–9

RUPERT
and Santa's Sneezes

It's Christmas Eve and Rupert is out in the garden making a snowman, when he hears the sound of an aeroplane. 'It's the Little Cowboy – I wonder what he can want?' he thinks.

As soon as the 'plane has landed the Little Cowboy jumps out. 'It's Santa,' he gasps, 'he's got the most terrible cold and can't get out of bed!' 'Oh no!' cries Rupert, 'that's awful – and it's Christmas Day tomorrow!' Explaining that, with Santa feeling so ill, there is chaos in his castle in the clouds, the Little Cowboy wonders if Rupert can come back with him to help. 'Of course,' agrees Rupert, and as soon as he has told his parents, he climbs into the tiny 'plane and they take off into the clear blue sky.

The moment the 'plane lands, Rupert and the Little Cowboy rush straight to Santa's bedroom. There, tucked up in bed, is Santa, looking very poorly. 'Atchooo!' he sneezes. 'Hadow Ruberd, I dowd dow wad do do, I can'd seem to stob sneezig.' 'He can't stop sneezing!' explains an elf. 'Thad's wad I sed! Atchoo!' says Santa, blowing his nose. 'You sound awful!' Rupert says, looking worried.

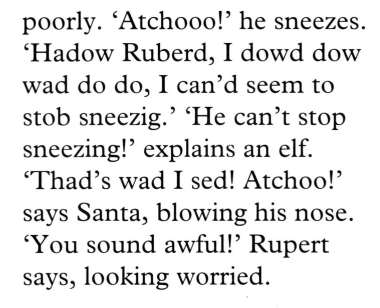

The pals go to the kitchens to see what is going on. 'We've boiled things up,' says the Little Cowboy, 'we've ground things down, 'we've mixed and we've mashed, but it's no good. If a cure for Santa isn't found soon the children won't get their presents!'

While the two pals are in the kitchen, Rika, the little Lapp girl who looks after Santa's reindeer, comes in. 'Hello Rupert,' she says, 'thank goodness you're here – you'd better come to the factory, everything's going wrong without Santa in charge!'

'Crikey!' exclaims Rupert, as they walk into the workshop. 'What's happening here?' All around them is a jumble of half-completed toys, with busy workers making more and more mistakes. Suddenly Rupert has an idea, 'My Uncle Bruno is a doctor, I'm sure he'll have a cure for Santa's sneezes!' Turning to the Little Cowboy he asks: 'Could you take me back to Nutchester straight away?' 'Follow me!' says the Little Cowboy.

Moments later they have taken off and are soon landing near Uncle Bruno's house. 'Santa's got an awful cold!' shouts Rupert as the two frier run across the snow to meet hi

'I'm sure there must be something in one of my book for sneezes,' he says. 'Ah yes! The very thing!' Quickly mixing all the ingredients, Uncle Bruno makes a guaranteed cure for Santa's cold. But then, when the Litt Cowboy tries to start his 'plar nothing happens! 'What'll we do?' he moans, 'We'll *never* get back in time now 'I'll call Rika and she can come on a reindeer for me! says Rupert. 'I'm leaving right away!' says Rika, as soon as she hears the news.

In what seems like no time at all, Rika arrives at Uncle Bruno's and Rupert is once again on his way back to Santa's castle. 'I do hope your uncle's medicine works!' Rika says, 'we just can't manage without Santa!'

Flying through the winter sky, Rupert spots the castle in the clouds as it appears on the horizon. 'Well,' thinks Ruper crossing his fingers, 'it won't be long now before we know whether Uncle Bruno's medicine has done the trick!

Everyone stands still and watches as Rupert gives Sant[a] two spoons of the medicine. 'Well, how do you feel now?' asks Rika. 'Bring me my clothes!' beams Santa, 'Clea[n] my boots! Brush my beard! My, but I do feel better!'

Rupert and Rika run straight to Santa's room. 'We're back!' pants Rupert, 'and I've got the medicine!' 'Atchooo!' sneezes Santa, 'well duthig else has worged so far,' he snuffles, 'so I hobe your Ungle dows wod he's doing!'

Once again Santa is in charge! Instantly the factory becomes its old self and everyone, including Rupert, pitches in to help. 'I think we'll just about make it!' smiles Santa, as the finished toys are wrapped in coloured paper and then packed into sacks.

While Santa checks all the last minute details, Rupert helps get the reindeer ready. 'It's going to be a long night for them,' says Rika, 'so we'd better give them a good meal.' 'I could do with some food myself,' laughs Rupert, 'I've *never* worked so hard!'

With seconds to spare the last sack is loaded on the sleigh and the final strap tightened! 'We made it,' grins Santa, 'now we must get you home!' 'Well done Rupert!' calls Rika as they fly away. 'Hurrah!' cheer all the helpers.

'I can't thank you enough,' says Santa, once they have landed, and he hands Rupert a special gift. Then the sleigh takes off, 'Now all the children will get presents!' smiles Rupert, as he waves Santa goodbye.